W9-CBH-766

THOMAS & FRIENDS™
STEAM ENGINE STORIES
THREE THOMAS & FRIENDS ADVENTURES

Random House 🏠 New York

A Random House PICTUREBACK® Book

Photographs by Terry Palone and Terry Permane

Thomas the Tank Engine & Friends™

CREATED BY BRITT ALLCROFT

Based on The Railway Series by The Reverend W Awdry.
© 2008 Gullane (Thomas) LLC.

Thomas the Tank Engine & Friends and Thomas & Friends are trademarks of Gullane (Thomas) Limited.
Thomas the Tank Engine & Friends & Design is Reg. U.S. Pat. & Tm. Off.
HIT and the HIT Entertainment logo are trademarks of HIT Entertainment Limited.

www.randomhouse.com/kids/thomas   www.thomasandfriends.com

Library of Congress Cataloging-in-Publication Data
Thomas & friends: steam engine stories / photographs by Terry Palone and Terry Permane. — 1st ed.
p.   cm. "Thomas the Tank Engine & Friends" "A Random House Pictureback book" "Created by Britt Allcroft"
"Based on the Railway series by the Rev. W. Awdry"
Contents: The magic lamp — James gets a new coat — Thomas and the golden eagle.
ISBN 978-0-375-85626-6 (pbk.)
[1. Railroad trains—Fiction.] I. Palone, Terry, ill. II. Permane, Terry, ill. III. Awdry, W. IV. Title: Thomas and friends.
PZ7.T3694545 2008   [E]—dc22   2008009229

Printed in the United States of America   10 9 8 7 6 5   First Edition

HiT entertainment

• THE MAGIC LAMP •

Narrow-gauge engines work very hard! They puff and chuff all day up and down the hills.

One day, the winding gear that carried coal cars up and down the Incline broke!

The engines had to work extra hard, pulling heavy coal cars up and down the long, steep track. Until, at the end of the day, they could ease their aching axles.

That evening, Thomas puffed into the Transfer Yards. All the narrow-gauge engines were there. Thomas was delivering steel winches and wires to repair the broken Incline.

"Listen, Thomas!" hooted Rusty. "Skarloey's telling us a story from the hills."

"Long, long ago," began Skarloey, "there was an old engine called Proteus. His lamp was so bright you could see it for miles around. Proteus said it was a magic lamp. He promised that if any engine ever found the lamp, their wishes would come true."

"How would you know it was Proteus' lamp?" asked Duncan.

"First you feel a rush of wind whenever the lamp is near," Skarloey chuffed quietly. "Then you hear a strange creaking sound. And finally," he added, "you'll see it flicker on and off, off and on."

Peter Sam huffed loudly. "I don't believe there's a magic lamp!"

Soon all the steel winches and wires were loaded into Peter Sam's freight cars.

"I have work to do," huffed Peter Sam. "I'm a Really Useful Engine, not a Really Silly one. The Incline must be working by morning, so I won't be wasting my time looking for a silly magic lamp!" he tooted proudly.

And he steamed quickly away.

The moon was bright. Peter Sam huffed and puffed. "The magic lamp I know isn't true. It's just an old story and quite silly, too." Peter Sam clickety-clacked towards a junction.

Suddenly he felt a great rush of wind! His axles rattled and his couplings creaked!

"What's happening?" Peter Sam whistled. He was so surprised he puffed right past the junction . . . and up the wrong line, away from the Incline.

Peter Sam still didn't believe Skarloey's story about Proteus' magic lamp.

But then he heard a creaking sound . . . and his wheels began to wobble.

Up ahead, a light flickered off and on, on and off.

And then he saw! It was just the Fogman's lantern. It creaked and croaked as it swung outside his cabin.

Peter Sam felt better. He chuffed past. Peter Sam was now even further from the Incline.

"The magic lamp I know isn't true. It's just an old story and quite silly, too," he huffed quietly to himself.

Then suddenly there was another rush of wind . . . then a creaking sound . . . and finally a flickering light . . . on and off, off and on!

The wind, the creaking sound, and the flickering light! "Could it be Proteus' lamp?" thought Peter Sam.

Then he saw it! It wasn't Proteus' lamp!

It was the light from a campfire at the children's campground. And it was the trees that were creaking in the wind!

"I knew that all along!" sighed Peter Sam. But now he chuffed on even more slowly. . . .

Peter Sam was at the bottom of a steep hill, and now he was completely lost. He didn't know what to do.

"I wish I could find the Incline. And I wish I could be safe at home in the Sheds with the other engines. And I wish," Peter Sam puffed quietly, "I wish I could find Proteus' lamp. Perhaps then my wishes would come true!"

Suddenly he felt a rush of wind whip round his wheels!
Then he heard the strangest creaking, croaking sound.
And then he saw a flickering light that flashed on and off, off and on!
It came from the top of the hill!
Peter Sam gasped. "It must be Proteus' magic lamp!"

He knew he had to go up the hill and find it. The wind whirred and stirred . . . the sound became a *whoosh*ing and a *wheesh*ing . . . and the light flickered brighter and brighter.

Peter Sam puffed to the top of the hill . . .

. . . and there was Harold the Helicopter!
His blades made a wind that whirred and stirred.
The sound *whoosh*ed and *wheesh*ed as the blades spun around.
And Harold's bright light flickered. On and off, off and on!

Peter Sam was very surprised!
"Harold!" he gasped.

"Hello!" hummed Harold. "I was
dropping off some packages for the
hill farms. What are you doing?"

"I'm lost," Peter Sam said. "And
I'm going to be very late to deliver the
winches and wires to the Incline."

"No problem, old buddy. I'll show you
the way." And Harold took to the air. His
strong light shone brightly and showed Peter Sam
the right way to the Incline.

Later, on his way home, Peter Sam couldn't stop thinking about what
had happened. "Maybe," puffed Peter Sam quietly, "you don't have to *see*
the magic lamp for your wishes to come true. Maybe it's enough just to
believe in it."

·JAMES GETS A NEW COAT·

All Sir Topham Hatt's engines like to look clean, bright, and shiny. They love being washed down and having their brass polished until it gleams.

James was in the workshop being repainted. He was beside himself with joy. James thought being repainted meant he was special.

The workmen painted and polished for hour upon hour.

Then, with new paint shining, brass twinkling, and blacking blacked, James returned to Tidmouth Sheds.

"Look! Aren't I a beautiful red?" he asked the others. "No wonder Sir Topham Hatt thinks I'm special."

But Percy was worried. He wasn't being repainted. And he wasn't red.

"Does this mean Sir Topham Hatt doesn't think *I'm* special?" he asked.

"Looking splendid is not the same as being Really Useful," said Thomas firmly.

"But best of all is being Really Useful *and* looking splendid—like me," said James cheerfully.

Before Thomas could say anything else, James closed his eyes and fell happily asleep.

The next morning, all the engines were very busy.

Percy was working at the coal plant.

Thomas and Emily were taking passengers up and down the Branch Lines.

Gordon was pulling the Express.

Sir Topham Hatt came to see James. He told him to join Percy at the coal plant—at once. "The coal cars must reach Brendam Docks before the boat sails. So *no* dillydallying," he said.

"Yes, Sir," said James. And he set off at once.

But James didn't go straight to the coal plant. He decided to go by the canal instead. Then he could see himself in the water for yard after yard after yard. . . .

"Magnificent," he puffed.

James had forgotten what Sir Topham Hatt had said.

At the coal yard, Percy was working as hard as he could. But he was falling behind.

The line of freight cars was getting longer and longer, and the Yard Manager was getting crosser and crosser.

Where could James be?

James was still enjoying himself. But there was no one around to share his fun, so he headed for Wellsworth Station.

But as James pulled in to Wellsworth Station . . .

Gordon and the Express were pulling out. The passengers had gone.

"Bother!" said James. He was disappointed. And he left the station.

James headed straight for the Branch Lines.

James saw Thomas. "Look at me," he puffed. "Don't I look fine?"

"You should be at work," called Thomas.

But James didn't listen to Thomas. James was enjoying being James.

But Percy wasn't enjoying being Percy. He was trying his hardest, but the Troublesome Trucks were being very naughty. Poor Percy was almost worn out.

"What will happen to the order now?" cried the Yard Manager.

When James rolled into the coal plant, it was late in the afternoon. Percy was cross. So was the Yard Manager.

"To make up for lost time," he said, "you must take an extra-long line of coal cars to the Docks."

James was delighted. The Docks were always bustling with engines and people.

"It's the place to be seen," he said.

"The Troublesome Trucks are being very naughty," warned Percy, but James still wasn't listening.

James puffed along, looking forward to being seen, but the Troublesome Trucks were naughtier than ever. They rocked and rolled and crashed and bashed. James' face was soon covered in soot.

Going downhill, the Troublesome Trucks wiggled and giggled. James had to put his brakes on with a jolt. Coal tumbled out of the Troublesome Trucks, landing on James.

James was cross and biffed the Troublesome Trucks as hard as he could. More coal flew out!

Now James didn't want to be seen. He was as dirty as he had ever been, but on his way to the Docks, he kept passing his friends.

He passed Emily . . .

and Edward . . .

and Thomas.

Thomas thought the only red thing left on James was his face!

James trundled into Brendam Docks. He hoped no one would see him. But Gordon was at the Docks with the Express. He could not believe his eyes. He thought James was the grubbiest, grimiest, dustiest, dirtiest engine he had ever seen.

Percy arrived safely with the last of the coal cars. "I like your new coat of paint," he puffed cheekily. "You do look splendid."

James knew he should have listened. He didn't feel splendid anymore. But for the first time all day, James could *hear* clearly. He could hear the sound of the Troublesome Trucks giggling at him.

And, despite feeling foolish, even James had to smile.

· THOMAS AND THE GOLDEN EAGLE ·

There are many different animals on the Island of Sodor. There are deer, cows, and sheep, and lots of beautiful birds.

One morning, Sir Topham Hatt came to Tidmouth Sheds. "A golden eagle has been seen at Bluffs Cove," he said. "It is a very special bird. Bird-watchers are coming from far and wide."

Thomas and Percy both wanted to take the bird-watchers to Bluffs Cove and see the golden eagle. But Sir Topham Hatt chose Emily.

"Percy, you are to collect milk from the Dairy," said Sir Topham Hatt. "And, Thomas, you are to collect stone from the quarry. It must reach Brendam Docks before the boat sails." Sir Topham Hatt left.

Thomas and Percy were disappointed. "I wish I was taking the bird-watchers," Percy said sadly.

"And I wish I could see the golden eagle," huffed Thomas as he set off.

Thomas arrived at the quarry. There were freight cars of stone as far as the eye could see.

"Cinders and ashes!" gasped Thomas, but he soon buffered up and puffed slowly away.

Thomas had to stop at the junction to Bluffs Cove.

Percy was waiting there.

They both watched as Emily cheerfully chuffed past. Her cars were filled with happy bird-watchers.

"I wish I could go up to Bluffs Cove," Percy puffed.

Then Thomas had an idea. Percy liked ideas.

"My train is long and heavy," puffed Thomas. "If you take half of my freight cars to the Docks before you go to the Dairy, I can go and find the golden eagle."

Percy listened carefully.

"Then I will collect the other half of my freight cars, and it will be your turn to go and see the eagle."

Percy thought this was a grand idea.

Thomas shunted his freight cars into the siding.

"It will be quicker to take half of the freight cars to Brendam Docks," Thomas said happily to Percy. And he headed for Bluffs Cove.

Percy buffered up to the train and puffed slowly away with half of Thomas' freight cars.

Thomas arrived at Bluffs Cove in no time at all.

He waited and waited. He was sure the golden eagle would come.

But the golden eagle was nowhere to be seen.

Thomas was disappointed. Then Bertie the Bus pulled up! "The golden eagle has been seen on Gordon's Hill!" he called.

"How exciting! I must get there right away!" cried Thomas, and he set off for Gordon's Hill at once. Thomas was so excited about seeing the golden eagle, he couldn't think of anything else.

He forgot about the freight cars full of stone . . .

. . . and he forgot about Percy.

Percy had taken half of Thomas' freight cars to the Docks. Now he headed for the Dairy to deliver the milk. He was happy. He'd have time to see the golden eagle.

But when Percy passed the siding near Bluffs Cove, he was surprised to see Thomas' half of the freight cars still there!

"If the boat sails without them, Thomas will be in trouble," worried Percy. Percy decided to help his friend.

Percy buffered up to the long line of freight cars and slowly puffed away.

Percy got to the Docks just in time. The quarry wagons were uncoupled and Percy set off again for the Dairy. He was feeling very tired.

Thomas was feeling full of puff.

He *wheesh*ed happily up Gordon's Hill. He was sure now he would see the golden eagle!

Thomas watched and waited . . . waited and watched. But the eagle didn't come. "I'll never see the golden eagle!" Thomas said sadly.

Suddenly Thomas remembered his cars of stone and Percy!

"Cinders and ashes," he cried, and he steamed off to the siding as fast as he could. But he didn't find his freight cars.

He found Percy! He was stuck in a siding—and he had not taken the milk to the Dairy.

"I took all your freight cars to Brendam," peeped Percy. "But now I have run out of coal!"

Thomas realized that now Percy couldn't see the golden eagle. And it was all his fault!

Bertie the Bus tooted excitedly. "The golden eagle has been seen back down the line," he called. "Hurry, Thomas!"

But Thomas knew what he must do. "I must take the milk to the Dairy," cried Thomas, "or Percy will be in trouble!"

The Dairy Manager was waiting when Thomas arrived. He delivered the fresh milk, just in time. Then he set off to rescue Percy.

Together, Thomas and Percy puffed slowly to the coal depot. But on the way, they were astonished to see—there, high on the rocks—not one, but two golden eagles. Thomas and Percy watched the two beautiful birds.

"Seeing two golden eagles is a wonderful thing," puffed Percy.

"But not as wonderful as helping a friend," said Thomas.

And they both happily agreed.